More Than One

By
Miriam Schlein
Pictures by
Donald Crews

SCHOLASTIC INC.
New York Toronto London Auckland Sydney

ISBN 0-590-10734-8

Text copyright © 1996 by Miriam Schlein.
Illustrations copyright © 1996 by Donald Crews.
All rights reserved. Published by Scholastic Inc., 555 Broadway, New York, NY 10012, by arrangement with Greenwillow Books, a division of William Morrow & Company, Inc.

SCHOLASTIC and associated logos are trademarks and/or registered trademarks of Scholastic Inc.

12 11 10 9 8 7 6 5 4 3 2 1   7 8 9/9 0 1 2/0

Printed in the U.S.A.   08
First Scholastic printing, September 1997

Watercolors and gouache paints were used for the full-color art.
The text type is Akzidenz Grotesk BE Super.

ONE
is
1

ONE sun
in the sky.

ONE whale in the water. **Can ONE be more than 1?**

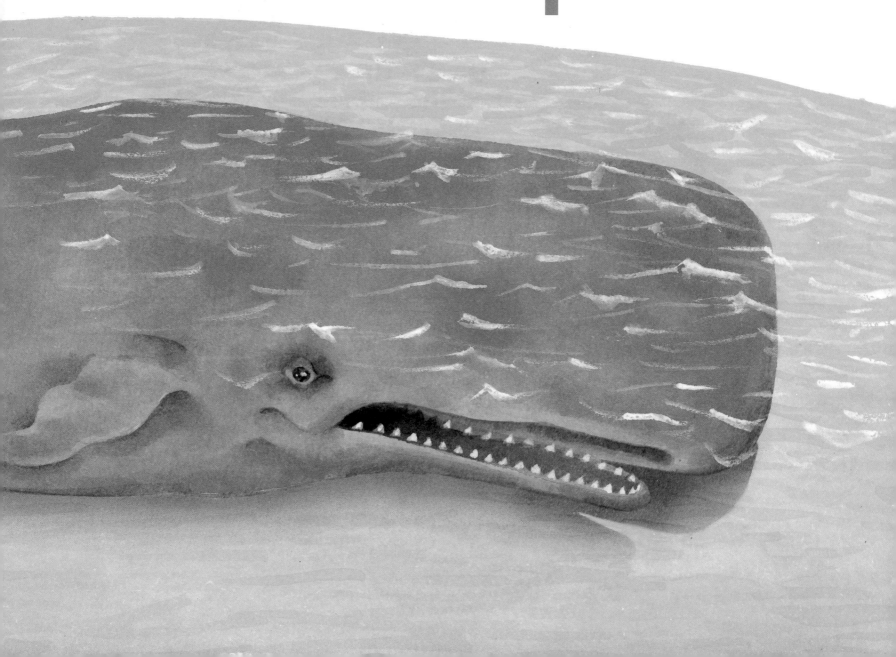

YES!

Here is **ONE PAIR** of shoes.

How many shoes in **ONE PAIR** of shoes?

ONE PAIR of shoes is **TWO SHOES.**

2

Whether they're on your feet or under the bed— a pair is always two. 2

Can ONE be more than that?

YES! **ONE WEEK is SEVEN DAYS.**
7

Can ONE be more than that?

One right after the other.

MONDAY 1
TUESDAY 2
WEDNESDAY 3
THURSDAY 4
FRIDAY 5
SATURDAY 6
SUNDAY 7

YES! **ONE BASEBALL TEAM is NINE PLAYERS.**

9

Count them.

Can **ONE** be more than that?

**YES!
ONE DOZEN
eggs is
TWELVE.**

12

**Twelve eggs.
Twelve eggs
all together.**

Can **ONE** be different, different every time?

YES! ONE FAMILY can be TWO PEOPLE, 2

THREE PEOPLE,
3

FOUR PEOPLE,
4

or FIVE,
5

or SIX,

6

or more.
How many
in your
family?

ONE FLOCK
of birds
can have
lots of birds.

It's awfully
hard to
count
them.

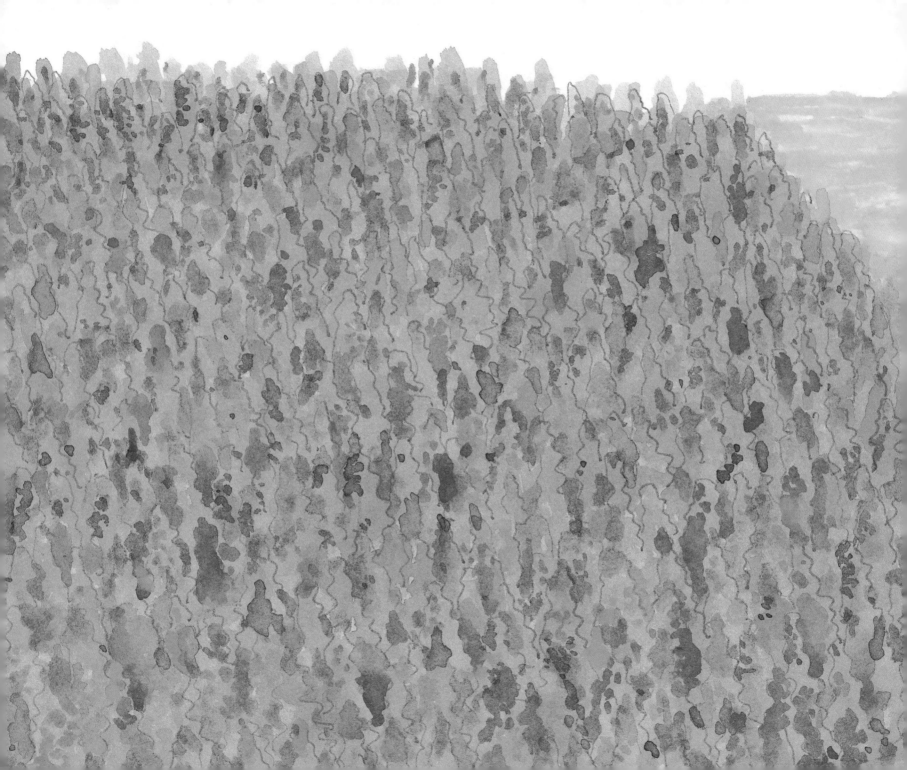

ONE FOREST
has lots of
trees.

ONE OCEAN
has billions
and trillions
and skadillions
of drops of water.

But they are still just
ONE FLOCK,
ONE FOREST,
ONE OCEAN.

ONE SCHOOL
of fish or

ONE CROWD
of kids is made
up of lots more
than one.

And
ONE BEACH
can have
so many
bits of sand,
you couldn't
count them
even if you sat
there counting
for a day,
a week,
a month,
or even a year....

ONE,
TWO,
THREE,
FOUR.
ONE can be **1**
and
ONE can be
more.